JASMINE'S
PARLOUR DAY

Lynn Joseph   *Ann Grifalconi*

Lothrop, Lee & Shepard Books   New York

For all the happy times I've spent on Maracas Beach—
with my brother, Gerard, who loves the doubles;
my sister, Christine, who loves the waves;
my cousin, Derek, who has helped me eat many bags
of poulari balls, red mangoes, and sugar cakes;
and especially my dad, Leslie, who will always
take me there.

L.J.

First Edition   1   2   3   4   5   6   7   8   9   10

Library of Congress Cataloging in Publication Data was not available in time for
the publication of this book, but can be obtained from the Library of Congress.
Jasmine's Parlour Day. ISBN 0-688-11487-3. — ISBN 0-688-11488-1 (lib. bdg.).
Library of Congress Catalog Card Number: 93-80196.

The sun climbs over the last green hill. It rounds the corner of Jasmine's house and shines through her window like it means business.

"Jasmine," it calls. But it sounds like Mama's voice. "Is Parlour Day, you forget?"

Jasmine jumps up fast fast. Her feet tangle up in the covers.

"I coming, Mama," she shouts, pulling her feet free. Jasmine hurries and washes her face. She plaits her hair tightly. Then she pulls on her red parlour dress and smiles.

Mama is standing in the doorway ready to go. She balances her big straw basket on her head like an angel with a heavy halo. Jasmine can smell the fishiness of the fresh fish in the basket.

"Can I carry de sugar cakes?" she asks.

Mama smiles. "As long as you don't eat any on de way."

Jasmine runs to the kitchen for the large batch of
sugar cakes. They will sell fast. Faster than the fish.
Then Mama and Jasmine set out for the market.

Jasmine tries to carry her basket of sugar cakes on her head, just like Mama. But she has to stick her arms up for balance. The basket keeps slipping— first to one side, then the other.

As she walks, Jasmine sees coconut trees, bread-fruit trees, and two iguanas sitting on a rock. The iguanas are hard to see because they look just like the rock.

Soon Mama and Jasmine arrive at their wooden parlour. It is at the side of the road and Maracas Bay gleams across the way.

"De sky blue for so," Jasmine says, looking up past the coconut trees. "Plenty people go want to come play at de beach today."

"Let us hope they want plenty fish and cakes, too,"
says Mama. She rests her basket down on the wide
blue counter.

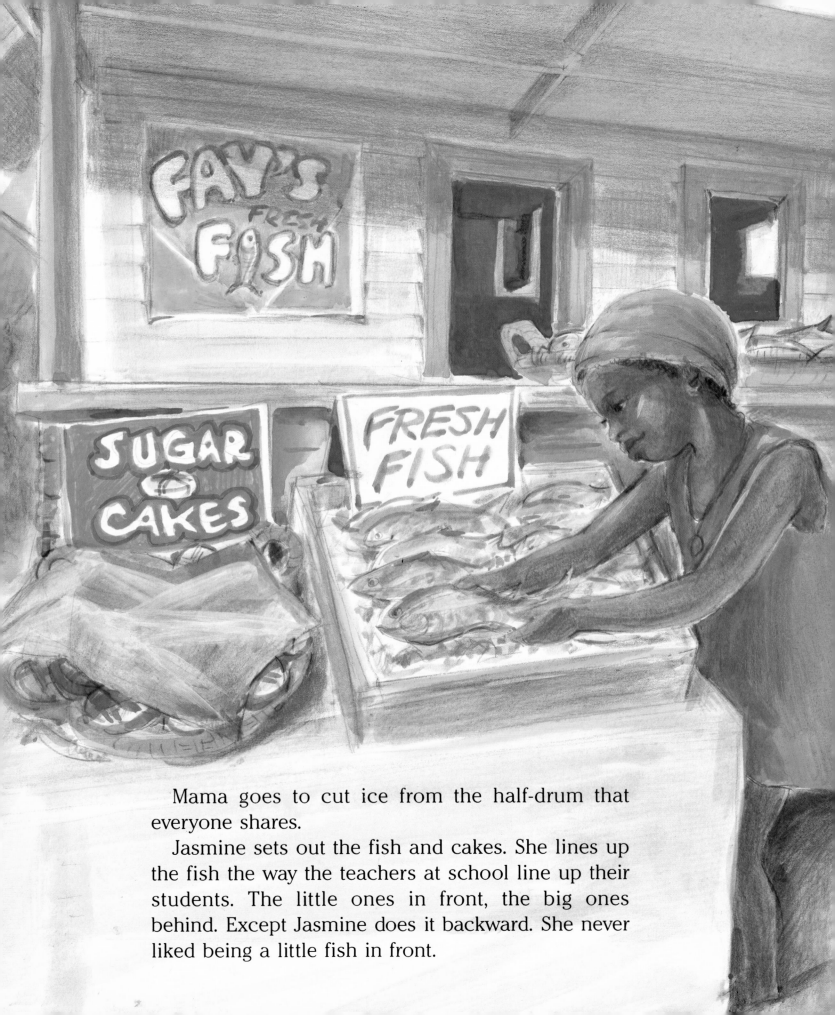

Mama goes to cut ice from the half-drum that everyone shares.

Jasmine sets out the fish and cakes. She lines up the fish the way the teachers at school line up their students. The little ones in front, the big ones behind. Except Jasmine does it backward. She never liked being a little fish in front.

When Mama comes back, she and Jasmine place
ice around the fish. Then Mama hangs the scale and
brings out two wooden crates for them to sit on.

But Jasmine isn't ready for selling yet. She can hear her friends shouting in the other parlours. She wonders what kind of good things to eat they will be selling today. She eyes the sugar cake basket.

"Can I take a sugar cake now, Mama?"

"Take some to share with your friends, too," Mama says with a little smile. "I know that's where you off to. But no skylarking," she warns. "We may have plenty selling to do."

Jasmine reaches under the cloth and pulls out two large pink sugar cakes. She breaks off an edge and puts it on her tongue. It's too sweet to bite into. She puts the sugar cakes in a bucket and carries it carefully on her arm.

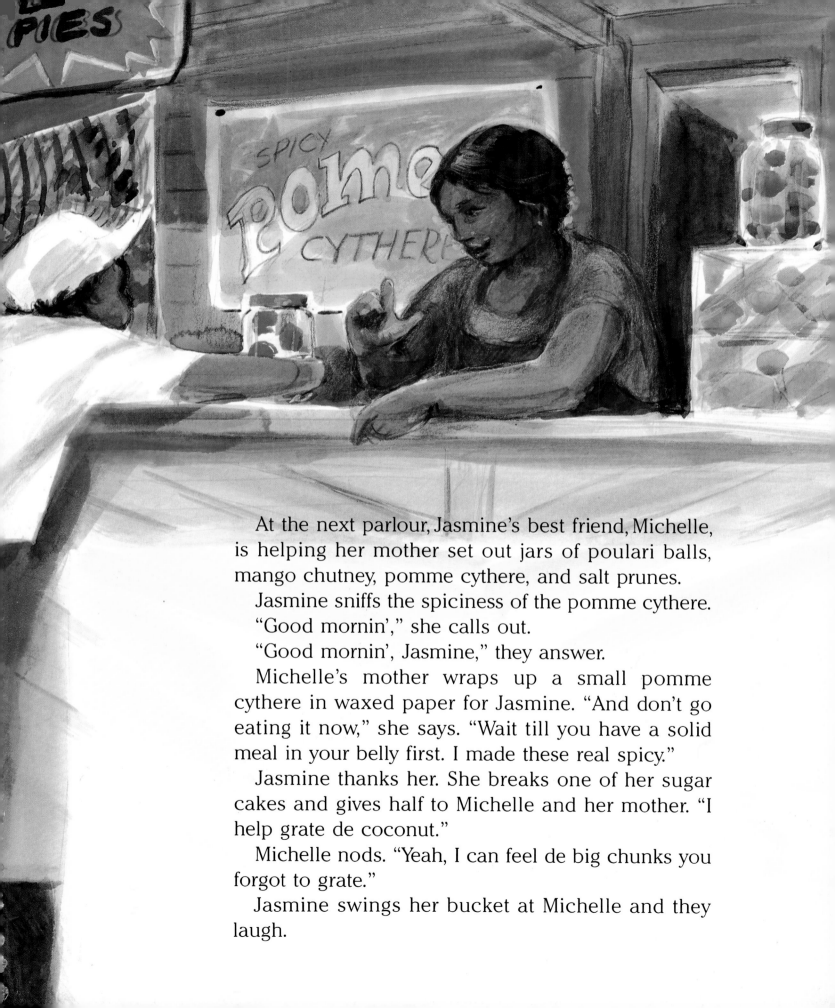

At the next parlour, Jasmine's best friend, Michelle,
is helping her mother set out jars of poulari balls,
mango chutney, pomme cythere, and salt prunes.

Jasmine sniffs the spiciness of the pomme cythere.
"Good mornin'," she calls out.

"Good mornin', Jasmine," they answer.

Michelle's mother wraps up a small pomme
cythere in waxed paper for Jasmine. "And don't go
eating it now," she says. "Wait till you have a solid
meal in your belly first. I made these real spicy."

Jasmine thanks her. She breaks one of her sugar
cakes and gives half to Michelle and her mother. "I
help grate de coconut."

Michelle nods. "Yeah, I can feel de big chunks you
forgot to grate."

Jasmine swings her bucket at Michelle and they
laugh.

The parlours begin to bustle as people shout hellos and visit each other. Jasmine hears "Taste de roti!" and "Get your shark 'n bake here!"

As soon as Michelle finishes helping, Jasmine grabs her hand and they set out to see who else has come to market.

"Look! There's Marcus polishing conch shells," Michelle shouts. She points to a tall bamboo table loaded down with heavy conches from the bottom of the sea.

Jasmine and Michelle run over to look at the smooth pink shells.

"Can we listen, Marcus?" they beg.

Marcus smiles. He gives them each a grandfather conch to press against their ears.

"I hear de sea," says Michelle.

"Me, too," says Jasmine. "This must be de singing of de sea that island fairies dance to."

They give Marcus back his shells and pretend they
are island fairies twirling from parlour to parlour.
They bump into each other and fall on the ground
laughing, right in front of mean old Miz Barrows,
who sits stirring her pot of crab and dumpling soup.
The girls smile at her.
"Humph!" she says to them, and continues stirring.

"Come on, Michelle," Jasmine says. She pulls her friend up, and they set off again. Derek is putting out his cold bottles of mauby, sorrel, and ginger beer. They stop to give him a piece of sugar cake.

"I'll come and play when I'm finished," he says. But since his sweet-drink parlour is the most popular at the beach, Derek never has time to play on Parlour Day. Jasmine gives him an extra piece of sugar cake, and they wave good-bye.

"Look at Carlos!" Michelle points to the next parlour. Carlos is juggling three red pommeracs. Oranges, grapefruits, guavas, soursops, mangoes, and pawpaws are lined up behind him like rainy-season rainbows.

Jasmine gives him half of the last sugar cake. "Can we juggle, too?" she asks.

Carlos takes a big bite of cake and nods his head. "But Mama only gave me these three pommeracs. They have bruises, so we not selling them."

Jasmine and Michelle take turns trying to juggle. Carlos gives advice as he sprinkles his fruits with water from a watering can.

The sun is rising higher in the sky. The parlour folks start putting up canvas shades and replacing ice around their wares. The black pitch road is glistening with heat. Jasmine and Michelle will have to put on slippers so their feet don't burn up.

Suddenly a car horn blares through the sound of the waves. Jasmine drops the pommeracs on the sand. Around the last green hill comes a line of cars. Some of the cars have surfboards on top. Some have beach balls in the windows. As they get closer, Jasmine hears loud calypso music from the car radios. The cars slow down and stop at the parlours.

Jasmine remembers Mama's words: "No skylarking." She picks up the pommeracs and gives them
to Carlos.

"Come on, Michelle. Parlour Day starting!"

As they race back to their parlours, Jasmine hears half of a sugar cake bumping about in her bucket. She stops to take it out. Right in front of mean Miz Barrows, who is still stirring her crab and dumpling soup.

Before Jasmine can think twice about it, she hands the sugar cake to Miz Barrows.

"Humph," the old woman says. But Jasmine is sure it's a nicer humph than before. She waves and runs to catch up with Michelle.

As Jasmine gets closer to her parlour, she sees Mama wrapping up fish and sugar cakes for customers. Her yellow apron flaps in the sea breeze. All around her, Jasmine hears the sounds of Parlour Day—

"Ice-cold drinks for de heat!" "Scrumptious crab soup to fill your belly!" "Sip sweet coconut water here!" "Mangoes, pawpaws—straight from de tree!"

And Jasmine joins in at the top of her voice—
"Sweet sugar cakes! Fresh fish! Right here!"